Don't Count Your Chickens

Don't Count Your Chickens

and Other Fabulous Fables

Mark Cohen

Illustrated by Mark Southgate

VIKING KESTREL

VIKING KESTREL

Published by the Penguin Group
27 Wrights Lane, London W8 5TZ, England
Viking Penguin Inc., 40 West 23rd Street, New York, New York 10010, USA
Penguin Books Australia Ltd, Ringwood, Victoria, Australia
Penguin Books Canada Ltd, 2801 John Street, Markham, Ontario, Canada
L3R 1B4
Penguin Books (NZ) Ltd, 182–190 Wairau Road, Auckland 10, New Zealand

Penguin Books Ltd, Registered Offices: Harmondsworth, Middlesex,
England

First published 1989

1 3 5 7 9 10 8 6 4 2

Filmset in Bembo by
Rowland Phototypesetting (London) Ltd

Printed and bound in Great Britain by
Butler & Tanner Ltd, Frome and London

A CIP catalogue record for this book is available from the British Library

ISBN 0-670-80951-9

Contents

ACKNOWLEDGEMENTS

The author and publisher gratefully acknowledge the following for their kind permission to include copyright material in this book:

Faber and Faber Ltd for 'How the Polar Bear Became' by Ted Hughes, from *How the Whale Became and Other Stories*; Jan Knappert for his story 'The Baboon and the Tortoise' from *Myths and Legends of the Swahili* (Heinemann African Writers Series); David Mackay for his retelling of 'The Faithful Tiger', from *A Treasury of Chinese Literature*, edited by Raymond Van Over (Random House Inc.); Frederick Warne for 'The Tale of Johnny Town-Mouse' by Beatrix Potter; Octagon Press Ltd and the author for 'The Man and the Tiger' by Idries Shah, from *Reflections*; Blackie & Son Ltd for 'Moving Day' by Roger Squire, from *Wizards and Wampum – Legends of the Iroquois*; Hamish Hamilton and Rosemary A. Thurber for 'The Fox and the Crow – Again', from *Further Fables of Our Time*, first published by Simon and Schuster, copyright © 1956 James Thurber and copyright © 1984 Helen Thurber.

Every effort has been made to trace copyright holders, but in a few cases this has proved impossible. The editor and publishers apologize for these cases of unwilling copyright transgression and would like to hear from any copyright holders not acknowledged.

What's a Fable?

Years and years ago, someone thought up a clever way of telling other people the truth without being rude. You made up a good story, often about animals. It might seem funny, but it was serious underneath. They called it a fable. The animals did some clever or silly things. But they were really the clever and silly things people do. So you might listen to a story and say to yourself: 'That fable's about me!' But no one *said* it was about you, so you didn't need to get angry. You'll see what I mean:

> There were once two tall mountains. Each with a castle on the top. In the valley between them a very hungry dog was chasing around trying to smell out a bird or a mouse to eat. Suddenly, a trumpet blew in one of the castles. This meant dinner was ready. The dog started up the mountain, thinking: 'There may be a few scraps going!' When he was only half-way up, the

trumpet stopped. Just then, another trumpet sounded from the other castle.

'They'll have finished their food here,' thought the hungry dog, 'by the time I arrive. But they're only just starting dinner over at the other one.' So he dashed down and started up the next-door mountain. But before he was half-way up, the first trumpet blew again. And the second one stopped. The dog rushed down the second mountain, and panted up the first, but ... He went on dashing up and down until both the trumpets had stopped and dinner was over in both castles. He didn't get any food.

Can you guess why someone thought of telling this doggy fable? And can you think of anyone who becomes worn out, dashing backwards and forwards – but never getting anywhere?

Hans Christian Andersen

Don't Count Your Chickens

When she had finished milking the cows, Mary swung the churn on to her head and set off for market. While she was walking, she made her plans.

'I should get enough from selling this milk to buy twenty boxes of eggs. With those I've saved already, that's nearly three hundred. Some of them will go bad, of course, before they hatch, and the rats may get a few. But I should have two hundred and fifty chicks, at least. They should be the right size to fetch the best price in the market. That should give me – let's see – seventy-five to spend. That'll certainly pay for a new dress. Now, what colour should it be? Yellow – no! Green – well, I do look good in green, though I say it myself. So, I'll settle for something green and silky-looking. That would be just right for the New Year's Eve dance. I shouldn't be short of partners – they'll fall over themselves, I'll be looking so good.

But I'm not going to dance with just anyone. I'll look them over, and shake my head if I don't fancy them.'

And in her day-dream that's exactly what she did. She tossed her head as proudly as though it were New Year's Eve already. But unfortunately that jolted the churn – and all the milk was spilt. And that was goodbye to the money, goodbye to the eggs, goodbye to the chicks – and goodbye to the green dress.

Aesop

Two Ways of Cooking the Goose

Two brothers were out hunting one day when they caught sight of a wild goose flying high above them. The elder brother fitted an arrow to his bow. 'Leave this one to me!' he shouted. 'If I hit it, it should cook a treat. I fancy it stewed with dumplings and red cabbage.'

'Hold on a minute!' said his younger brother. 'It would taste far better roasted. You know how I like the crisp skin and stuffing.'

'I'm older and what I say goes,' answered his brother sharply.

'Why are you so obstinate? You always want your own way,' grumbled the younger one.

'And you're spoilt!' snapped his brother. The squabble rumbled and grumbled between them, for neither would give way. In the end they decided they would have to ask their grandfather, who was old and wise, and was used to his grandsons disagreeing.

'What's the best way of cooking the goose, grandpa?' they asked him. After careful thought the old man advised them to stew the goose to start with, then stuff it and put it in the oven. The two brothers thought about this, went on arguing for a little, but in the end agreed to the old man's plan.

Then they went back to the spot where they had sighted the goose – but, of course, it had flown off long ago.

Traditional Chinese

The Goose that Laid Golden Eggs

There was once a man who was lucky enough to own a miraculous goose. Every day of its life, without fail, it laid a shining egg of solid gold. Most people would have been satisfied with having a golden egg every single day, but this man was impatient and greedy. 'Why wait?' he said to himself. 'The bird must be so full of golden eggs that I could be the richest man in the world and never have to worry again.' So he killed the golden goose and cut her open. But instead of a hoard of treasure, he found that she was exactly the same inside as any ordinary goose – only dead!

Aesop

The Ugly Duckling

Once upon a time there was a mother duck who had been sitting patiently on her eggs for a long while. At last they hatched, all except the last one – and it was bigger than all the others. 'I expect it's a turkey egg,' said an old duck who knew about these things.

When the last egg hatched, out came a tiny bird. It did not look like the other ducklings. But at least it wasn't a turkey. For next day it took to the water and swam as well as all the others. 'He's not so ugly when you take a close look at him,' said the mother duck.

But none of the other birds in the farmyard agreed. Every one of them either chased the poor duckling or nipped him or bullied him. Even his own brothers and sisters. They were horrid to him, and kept quacking: 'If only the cat would get you, you ugly thing.' He was so ugly that even his mother could not treat him like all her other children. He felt ashamed – as though it were his own fault that he was ugly.

At last the duckling could bear the insults no longer.

He escaped and flew away to the swamp where the wild ducks lived.

'You *are* ugly,' said the wild ducks, 'but that isn't our business, as long as you are not planning to make a nest and settle in with us.' But all the duckling really wanted was to live in peace.

Alas, the hunters did not leave the ducks in peace. A whole crowd of them trampled through the reeds. Their guns shattered the air. Their bitter blue smoke lay over the water. Many of the birds were killed. The duckling was terrified and hid his head under his wing. When at last the shooting stopped, he ran away again. He found a tumbledown hut where an old woman lived with a cat and a hen. She locked him up: 'I'll keep this ugly duckling for a week or two. Perhaps it will start to lay. That would make a change from hens' eggs.' Of course, she did not know that he was a drake, that is a boy duck. He hated being cooped up and became sadder every day. He longed to be in the open air, floating on the water.

'Why are you so miserable?' asked the hen. 'You have nothing to do, that's why you get these odd ideas into your head. If you learned to lay eggs like me, or purr like pussy over there, you would stop worrying.'

But the ugly duckling was not clever enough to lay eggs or to purr. So he decided to escape into the wide world.

'Please yourself,' said the hen with a sniff.

He found a lake where he could float in the water and dive to the bottom. But still all the other ducks ignored him because he was so ugly.

Autumn was coming; the evenings were getting chilly, and the wind whipped the yellow and brown leaves from the trees. At sunset one evening, a flock of magnificent birds with gleaming white feathers and long graceful necks appeared on the lake. The swans were on their way south to a warmer country where the lakes did not freeze in winter. As they circled higher and higher in the sky, the ugly duckling swam round and round on the lake, stretching his neck towards them. A strange sad feeling came over him, and a strange sad cry came from his throat. Those beautiful birds looked so happy.

The winter grew colder and colder, and gradually the ice closed in upon the duckling. At last he was too tired to go on swimming and the ice gripped him tight.

Early the next morning a farmer saw him, broke the ice, and carried the frozen bird home to his wife. She brought him back to life. Her children tried to play with him, but the duckling took fright, tumbled into the milk, the butter, and even the flour. The farmer's wife shouted angrily at him, for he was making a terrible mess. But her children rolled about with laughter, for he was making a *lovely* mess. Round and round the kitchen they chased him, until at last he was able to escape once more into the frozen world outside.

Somehow the poor duckling lived through the long harsh winter. When at last spring came to the swamp, he spread his wings and took off into the sweet air. His wings felt wide and strong as he swept over green gardens and orchards bright with blossom. Suddenly three magnificent swans swam out of a forest of rushes. As he saw again those royal snow-white birds, the ugly duckling felt the same strange sadness he had known the autumn before.

'I am going to fly over to them,' cried the poor bird. 'I know I'm ugly, but what have I got to lose? I'd rather be beaten by them than nipped by ducks or pecked by hens, or suffer in the farmyard or freeze through the long winter as I have done.'

He flew down to the water and swam bravely towards those proud birds. And they swam towards him. He humbly bowed his head, for he was expecting them to attack him as everyone else had done. But

18

what did he see in the water? It was his own reflection. He was no longer a clumsy, ugly grey bird. *He* was a swan! All his pain and suffering seemed worthwhile as the swans swam round him and greeted their new brother joyfully.

As the children came through the garden with bread for the swans, the youngest cried: 'Just look at that new one! Isn't it the most beautiful of all?' Though he couldn't believe his happiness, the ugly duckling was now the most beautiful swan. And swans are the most beautiful birds in all the world!

Hans Christian Andersen

The Ant and the Grasshopper

It was a frosty day in the middle of winter. The busy ant was dragging out the corn, grain by grain, which he had stored away in the summer. It had got wet, so he laid it out to dry. The grasshopper was half-dead with hunger. He begged the ant for a little corn to keep body and soul together.

'Why didn't you collect some and store it during the summer, like me?' said the ant crisply.

'Well,' replied the grasshopper, 'I really hadn't the time. I was far too busy.'

'Too busy doing what?' asked the ant.

'Singing, naturally! Grasshoppers have to sing all summer.'

'Lucky old you. I didn't have a moment. It was work, work, work.' And the ant laughed as he firmly closed the door of his store-room. 'Well, if you had the time to sing all summer, you are going to have plenty of time to dance all winter!'

Aesop

The Crow and Her Children

When her children were old enough, Mother Crow called them together to teach them how to look after themselves in the hard world outside their nest.

'Children, don't be rash or too sure of yourselves. Beware of human beings, especially when you see one bend down and pick up a stone.'

'What should we do, mother,' asked one of the youngsters, 'if we see one with a stone already in his hand?'

'Dear children,' replied Mother Crow, 'if you can ask a question like that, it shows you are already very careful. So you won't come to much harm.'

Traditional Armenian

The Fox and the Crow

One day a crow flew in at a kitchen window and stole a large chunk of cheese. Off she flapped to a tall tree, and settled down to enjoy her delicious meal. But a sharp-eyed and quick-witted fox was passing. He looked up and saw the crow – and the cheese.

'Dear lady, how wonderful you're looking. How glossy and black your wings are. How bright and gleaming your eyes! What's the eagle got – and he's supposed to be the king of birds – that you haven't got? It just seems so unfair that you were not given a voice.'

The crow drank in every word of the fox's flattery, and smiled to herself. For she knew she could surprise him by showing she *had* a voice. She opened her beak to caw – but of course the cheese dropped out and fell straight into the fox's waiting jaws below. The fox ran off, delighted with his success.

'I made much of her beauty,' he said to himself, his mouth full of cheese, 'but I wouldn't say much for her brains!'

Aesop

The Fox and the Crow – Again

The crow in the tree with the cheese in his beak began singing, and the cheese fell into the fox's lap.

'You sing like a shovel,' said the fox with a grin. But the crow pretended not to hear and cried out: 'Quick, give me back the cheese! Here comes the farmer with his rifle!'

'Why should I give you back the cheese?' the wily fox demanded.

'Because the farmer has a gun – and I can fly faster than you can run.'

So the frightened fox tossed the cheese back to the crow, who ate it, and said: 'Dearie me, my eyes are playing tricks on me, or am I playing tricks on you? Which do you think?'

But there was no reply, for the fox had slunk away into the woods.

James Thurber

The Fox and the Stork

A fox one day met a stork who had flown in from abroad. 'You must come to see us while you're here,' said the fox in a welcoming voice. 'Let's fix a date. How about coming over to supper tomorrow night? That will give me time to prepare something a little special, just the sort of thing for a visitor.' The stork thought this was a very kind invitation, so of course she accepted. 'Grand, tomorrow night then, about half-past seven!' said the fox, and told the stork how to get to his house.

Next evening, sure enough, the stork arrived for dinner. The air was full of the delicious smell of food. 'Please come and sit down!' cried the fox, and brought out a large shallow bowl of thin soup. 'Do start, dear Mrs Stork.' And the fox began to lap up the liquid himself, smacking his lips and enjoying every mouthful.

The poor stork, with her long narrow bill, couldn't eat anything at all. She could only feel hungrier and hungrier, and angrier and angrier.

When the fox had licked up the last drop of soup, he looked up in mock surprise and said, 'But Mrs Stork, you've hardly eaten a thing. It must be my cooking. I am *so* sorry. I probably put too much salt in it for your taste.'

'No, no, it was delightful,' Mrs Stork replied. 'You're a very clever cook – it was just – that I wasn't really hungry.'

'But,' she said as she left, 'I do hope you're free tomorrow evening, because I'd so like to ask you back and cook you one of *our* specialities.' Of course the fox accepted her kind invitation, and promised to come.

Next evening he arrived to the most mouth-watering smells, and very soon Mrs Stork asked him to sit down to dinner. The supper was served in long narrow bottles.

'Do start,' said the stork kindly. 'You must be hungry as a hunter, Mr Fox!' But only she laughed at the joke, because he could see he was going to *stay* hungry. The stork stuck her long bill into a bottle and started eating with obvious enjoyment. The fox had to make do with the few drops that fell from the bottle.

'You've hardly touched a thing,' cried the stork when she had eaten her fill. 'It must be my cooking. Did I put too much pepper in it? Did it taste too sharp?'

'It's you who were too sharp,' said the fox – and went home hungry.

Aesop

Sour Grapes

There was once a fox who was dying of hunger. He couldn't even remember his last meal, for it was so long ago. As he was slinking past a vineyard, he caught sight of bunches and bunches of ripe, juicy-looking grapes. His mouth watered and his tummy rumbled. The vines had been trained up trees, so the grapes hung far above the fox's head. He stood on his hind legs but he couldn't reach the lowest bunch. He tried jumping, but still couldn't touch the grapes. Again and again he jumped, feeling weaker with each leap – but the bunches were just out of reach.

At last he had to give up. 'I'm not very bothered,' he said to himself as he went on his hungry way. 'I am sure they weren't ripe anyway. Those grapes looked very sour to me!'

Aesop

The Fox and the Tiger

A tiger who was out hunting for his next meal caught a fox. He was trying to make up his mind which end of the fox to start on, when the cunning animal said: 'My dear Mr Tiger, you surely can't be thinking of eating me?' The tiger admitted that that was just what he had been thinking of doing. 'But surely, you must know . . . ?' the fox went on.

The tiger racked his brains – but he couldn't remember any good reason for *not* eating foxes. They weren't poisonous to tigers, as far as he knew.

'Of course you can't eat me,' the fox explained patiently. 'The Emperor of Heaven has appointed me to be King of all the animals. So if you ate me that would be a terrible insult to the Emperor – who doesn't take kindly to anyone disobeying his orders.'

The tiger had heard nothing about the fox becoming King, and wasn't sure he believed the story.

'If you don't believe me, Mr Tiger, let me show you,' the fox said. 'Just follow me. You'll soon see how afraid all the other animals are of their King. Unless I am very much mistaken, they'll scatter as I approach.' The tiger agreed with this clever plan of the fox's. Indeed, every animal that caught sight of them *did* scurry away into the jungle in alarm. The silly tiger didn't realize that the animals were afraid of *him*, not of the fox at all. So the fox may not really have been the King of the animals – but he was clever enough to save his own life.

Traditional Chinese

The Man and the Tiger

A man being followed by a hungry tiger turned in desperation to face it, and cried: 'Why don't you leave me alone?'

The tiger answered: 'Why don't *you* stop being so appetizing?'

Idries Shah

The Faithful Tiger

Once there was an old woman who lived with her one and only son. He looked after her well. One day he went up to the hills near the town to cut bamboo. While he worked, a tiger crept out of the trees. It leapt upon him and ate him up.

When the old woman heard about her son's death, she was overcome with sadness. She wept bitterly and wished that she too might die.

'Oh my son, how am I to live without you?' she cried.

And in great distress, she set out to seek help from the local Magistrate. She stood before him and told her sad story. And when she had come to the end of it she demanded that the Magistrate arrest the tiger.

The Magistrate laughed.

'Arrest a tiger!' he exclaimed. 'How can I arrest a tiger?'

'Send your men up into the hills to find him,' said the old woman through her tears.

The Magistrate was upset by such a request and

began to lose his temper.

'I can't do that sort of thing,' he said. 'Go home, old woman.'

But the old woman would not. She wept even more and begged him to send his men out to arrest the tiger. At last the Magistrate felt so sorry for her, she was so old and so distressed, that he agreed to do what she asked.

'All right, all right,' he said. 'I will make an order for the arrest of the tiger and one of my men will go up into the hills to look for it. Now go home and rest, old woman. I will do all I can.'

The old woman was cheered by his words but she would not go home until she had seen the Magistrate write out the warrant for the tiger's arrest. He was not at all pleased at this. But he did not want to upset her, so he called his men together to ask which of them would go up into the hills to arrest the tiger.

Now one of them, a man called Yang Chu, had just come from a wedding feast, and was as drunk as a lord. This made him feel strong and brave. 'I will do it,' he said.

So the Magistrate signed the warrant for the tiger's arrest and gave it to Yang Chu. And the old woman went home.

The first thing that Yang Chu did then was to fall asleep. When he woke up, he remembered the warrant and he no longer felt strong and brave.

'Why was I so stupid? Why did I offer to go up into the hills to arrest a tiger? I must have been mad.'

But the more he thought about it, the more certain he was that the Magistrate did not expect him to do such a crazy thing.

'It was only a trick to get rid of the old woman,' he decided.

He began to feel strong and brave once more.

So he did nothing at all to find the tiger and after a

while he went to the Magistrate and gave him back the warrant.

But the Magistrate refused to take it.

'Oh no!' he said sternly. 'You offered to go up into the hills to arrest this tiger and I'm not letting you off now. You *must* do it.'

Yang Chu was frightened by the Magistrate's stern words. How on earth could he arrest a tiger all by himself? He begged the Magistrate to let him have some huntsmen to help him. When this was agreed, he collected them all together and led them up into the hills.

For a day and a night they searched and searched. But there was no sign of the tiger.

'Well, I tried to find it. Now I have done my duty,' said Yang Chu with relief. 'The tiger has disappeared.'

When he reported this, the Magistrate was furious and had him given a good beating. Yang Chu was ordered to continue the search all by himself. He spent many days up in the hills and not once did he catch sight of the tiger. Each time he returned, he was beaten for failing to do his duty.

After a month of this, Yang Chu could bear it no longer. Instead of going in search of the tiger, he went to the temple just outside the town. He fell to his knees and prayed for help. He wept too, because of all the trouble he was in.

After a while, a tiger walked in. This gave Yang Chu a terrible fright, and he thought: 'He will kill me too, just as he killed the old woman's son.' But the tiger just sat by the door of the temple and took no notice of anyone.

At last Yang Chu stood up and went to the tiger and said: 'Oh tiger, if it was you that killed the old woman's son, I beg you to let me tie this rope round your neck and take you to the Magistrate.' The tiger bent his head so that Yang Chu could do so and

32

together they walked through the town to the Magistrate's office.

Hearing what had happened, the old woman and all the Magistrate's men came to the office to learn how the tiger would be judged.

'Did you kill the old woman's son?' asked the Magistrate.

The tiger nodded.

'Well then, you are a murderer and the law says that you must die.'

The tiger listened politely to what the Magistrate was saying.

'Did you know that the old woman had only one son? You killed him and there is nobody to look after her in her old age.'

He paused and looked at the tiger.

'But,' he went on, 'if you will be a son to her and take care of her as her own son did, I will pardon your crime.'

The tiger nodded and the Magistrate ordered Yang Chu to set him free.

This made the old woman very angry. She felt that the tiger should have died for murdering her son.

She woke early next morning and opened the door of her cottage. There, lying in the path, was the body of a deer. She took a little of the meat for herself and sold the rest in the market. With the money she bought things that she needed. After this the tiger brought something for the old woman every day. Sometimes he brought her money and expensive things and it was not long before she had plenty of everything.

'He looks after me better than my own son did,' she said. She grew fond of the tiger and let him sleep by the door at night. Sometimes he stayed with her all day. Since his arrest the tiger had hurt no one.

Then one day the old woman died. There was enough money to give her a fine funeral with many flowers. When all her relatives and friends were standing around her grave, the tiger bounded out and everyone ran away. But he only went up to it and stood there roaring like thunder. Then he walked away and no one ever saw him again.

And when it was certain that he was not going to return, the people of the town built a shrine to honour the faithful tiger and it is still there.

Traditional Chinese, retold by David Mackay

The Shepherd Boy Who Cried Wolf

There was once a shepherd boy who loved playing practical jokes. He drove his sheep to a spot not too far out of the village, chose his moment, and then shouted at the top of his voice: 'Wolf, wolf! Help, help! They're attacking the sheep. For God's sake, come and help!'

The first time this happened all the villagers came rushing out in alarm. They brought sticks and stones to frighten off the wolves.

'Fooled you,' crowed the shepherd boy. 'It was only a joke. There aren't any wolves.'

He let some days pass, and then started yelling once more: 'Wolf, wolf! Help, help! They're attacking the sheep. For God's sake, come and help!'

Exactly the same thing happened. The villagers rushed to help.

A few weeks later, he got away with his trick a third time.

But soon after, a pack of wolves really did attack the

flock: 'Wolf, wolf! Help, help! They're attacking the sheep. For God's sake, come and help!'

'Here we go again,' said one villager to another. 'We've heard that one before. Pull the other leg.'

So they went on with what they were doing. The shepherd boy just had to look on, while the wolves ate every sheep in his flock.

Aesop

The Dog and the Shadow

A dog once stole a joint of meat from a butcher's shop. On her way home she had to cross the river. As she was scampering over the bridge, she saw a reflection of herself in the water below. She thought (because she was rather silly): 'This must be another dog!' And she thought (because she *was* rather a silly dog): 'This must be another joint of meat!' And she was *sure* that the joint of meat was larger and juicier than her own. She was so greedy that she wanted both of them for herself. So she dropped her own meat, snarled, and made a dash at the other joint. That way she ended up without any meat, and the joint ended up at the bottom of the river.

Aesop

The Dog in the Manger

Once upon a time there was a farm-dog who found his way into the stable, jumped into the manger, and made himself very snug in a bed of soft hay. When the horses came in after a long day's work in the fields, they were horribly hungry. They made straight for their manger, sniffing the delicious hay. But the dog was comfortable and did not like being disturbed.

'Would you move?' asked the horses politely. 'You're lying on our dinner, and we're so hungry we could eat a haystack.'

'Too bad,' answered the dog. 'I'm very comfortable, and I'm so tired I could sleep for a week.'

So the selfish dog lay on the hay – though of course *he* couldn't eat it. The horses stayed horribly hungry, and wished he would find somewhere else for a bed.

Aesop

The Cat and the Dog

Once upon a time a man called Simon and his wife Susan lived by the river with their old cat and dog. One day Simon said to Susan, 'Why should we keep that old cat any longer? She can't catch mice any more – in fact she's so slow she's no use to anyone. Why, a whole family of mice might dance on top of her and she wouldn't catch a single one. She's got to go. The next time I see her, I shall drown her in the river.'

Susan was very unhappy when she heard this, and so was the cat, who had been listening behind the stove. When Simon went off to his work, the poor cat miaowed pitifully and looked sadly up into Susan's face. So the woman quickly opened the door and said, 'Run away as fast as you can, puss – quick, before Simon comes home.'

The cat took her advice and ran as quickly as her poor old legs would carry her into the wood. When Simon came home, his wife told him the cat had vanished.

'So much the better for her,' said Simon. 'And now

that we're rid of her, we must think what to do with the old dog. He's deaf and blind and is for ever barking when there's no need, and not making a sound when there is. The courtyard might be swarming with thieves and he'd not raise a paw. The next time I see him, I'll hang him.'

When she heard this Susan was very unhappy, and so was the dog, who was lying in the corner of the room and had heard everything. As soon as Simon went off to work, the dog howled so miserably that Susan quickly opened the door, and said, 'Come on, dear, off you go, before Simon gets home.' And the dog ran into the wood. When her husband returned, Susan told him the dog had disappeared.

'Lucky for him,' growled Simon. But Susan was very unhappy, for she had been fond of both her pets, and now they were gone.

Now it happened that the cat and the dog met each other on their travels. Though they hadn't been the best of friends at home, they were glad to meet among strangers. They sat down under a holly tree and talked about how pleasant life had been back at the farm, and how they wished they were back at home. Presently a fox passed by and, seeing the pair together, asked them why they were sitting there and what they were grumbling about.

The cat replied, 'I've caught many a mouse in my day, but now that I'm too old to work, my master wants to drown me.'

And the dog said, 'I've watched and guarded my master's house night after night, and now that I'm too old and deaf, he wants to hang me.'

The fox answered, 'That is the way of the world. I think I can help you both to get back in front of your master's fire. But first, will you help me in *my* troubles?'

They promised to do their best, and the fox

explained. 'The wolf has declared war against me, and is at this very moment planning to attack me with the help of the bear and the wild boar. Tomorrow there will be a terrible battle.'

'All right,' said the dog and the cat. 'You can count on our help.' And they shook paws on the bargain. The fox sent word to the wolf to meet him at a certain place, and the three set forth to face him and his friends.

The wolf, the bear and the wild boar arrived first. They waited some time for the fox, until the impatient bear said, 'I'll climb that oak tree, and see if they're coming.'

The first time he looked round, he said, 'I don't see anything.' The second time he looked round, he said, 'I still don't see anything.' But the third time he roared with laughter and said, 'I can see a vast army in the distance, and one of the soldiers has the biggest spear I've ever seen!'

He had spied the cat, who was marching along with her tail on end. Then they all laughed and jeered; but it was so hot that the bear yawned and said, 'The enemy won't be here for hours, so I'll just curl up in the fork of this tree and take a little nap.'

The wolf lay down under the oak, and the wild boar buried himself in some straw so that you could only see one ear. And while they were lying there, the fox, the cat and the dog arrived. When the cat saw the wild boar's ear she pounced on it, thinking it was a mouse in the straw.

The wild boar scrambled up in a dreadful fright, gave one loud grunt, and disappeared into the wood. But the cat was even more startled than the boar. Spitting with terror, she sprang up into the fork of the tree and, as it happened, landed right in the bear's face. Now it was the bear's turn to be in a fright, and with a mighty growl he jumped from the oak, fell right on top of the wolf, and they were both killed. The fox was delighted. 'Right,' he said. 'Now it's time for me to keep *my* part of the bargain.'

On their way home the fox caught a mass of mice, and when they reached Simon's cottage he laid them in a row on the stove. 'Now take one mouse after another,' he told the cat, 'and lay them down in front of your master.'

She did exactly as the fox told her.

When Susan saw this, she said to her husband, 'Just look! Here's our old cat back again – and what a great number of mice she's caught!'

'Wonders will never cease!' cried Simon. 'I certainly never thought that old cat would ever catch another mouse.'

But Susan answered: 'There, you see, I always said she was a wonderful mouser – but you always think you know best.'

Then the fox said to the dog, 'Our friend Simon has just killed a pig and made a string of sausages that just asks to be stolen. When it's a little darker, slip into the courtyard and bark with all your might.'

'All right,' said the dog. And as soon as it was dusk he began to bark loudly.

Susan heard him first and called to her husband, 'Our dog must have come back, for I know his bark. Do go out and see what's the matter. Perhaps someone is stealing our sausages.'

But Simon answered: 'That silly animal's as deaf as a post and is always barking for nothing.' And he stayed put in his chair.

The next morning Susan rose early to go to the nearby town, and thought she would take some sausages to her aunt there. But when she went to her larder, she found all the sausages gone, and a great hole in the floor. She called out to her husband: 'There, I knew I was right. Thieves *were* here last night, and they haven't left a single sausage. Oh, if only you'd gone when I asked you to!'

Then Simon scratched his head and said, 'I don't understand it at all. I'd certainly never have guessed the old dog was so sharp of hearing.'

But Susan replied, 'Didn't I always tell you our old dog was a wonderful watchdog? – but as usual, you thought you knew best.'

So everyone was happy again. The cat curled up by the stove. The dog lay down in his special place in the corner. And the fox had eaten so many sausages he could eat no more.

Brothers Grimm

A Cat May Look at a King

Many years ago a not very wise King asked four animals to join his court: he put the bear in charge of his wars; the stag in charge of his post; the ape of his laws; the cat of his household. But the ape was jealous of the other animals and hatched a plan to disgrace them, so that only he remained in the King's favour.

'I wonder, your Royal Highness,' he said, 'if this idea of mine would amuse you this evening. You could ask each animal to perform a special trick. If you wrote down the instructions and gave them to all of us on the spot, we would not have a chance to practise. That would be most fair and most fun.'

'It is a splendid idea, Lord Ape, but I would not know what test to set each of you. *You* should think out the tasks in the competition. It is your idea, after all, and I am sure you will be as just as you always are in the law courts!'

This was just what the wily ape had hoped for, but he hummed and hawed before he said: 'If you insist –

but you must promise not to tell anyone that I, and not your Majesty, wrote the instructions.'

The cat sat silently under the royal throne, and heard every word. 'Hmmm,' he said to himself, 'I am not at all sure that our friend Lord Ape can be trusted. He's plotting something.' And he followed the ape to his room. Here the noble lord planned three impossible tasks for the other animals. He himself was only asked to make a low bow to the court – not very difficult. Because he was not very good at writing, the ape spelt out every word aloud. The cat heard everything through the keyhole, and crept away to make his own plans.

That night, all the animals gathered after supper. The King and his beautiful daughter, the Princess Squisita, took their seats. The King told everyone the plan.

Before he opened the first paper, though, the cat stepped forward. 'Your Majesty,' he said, 'I have heard your splendid idea for this evening. I will be only too pleased to take part. But might I suggest that you should give a small prize to any of us who carry out our task. On the other hand, if we fail, you should send us away from the court for ever.'

'That is an excellent idea – just what I had in mind,' answered the King, although he had not had it in mind. 'And if one of the other animals can carry out the task written on the paper, *he* shall win the prize.'

So the royal trumpet blew, the ape laughed to himself, and the stag came forward to hear the first instructions.

'To my Lord Stag: He must jump head-first from the golden balcony, and land before the throne.' The balcony was very high; the poor stag had long delicate antlers and long delicate legs. The jump would be suicide.

'I fear, your Majesty, that I cannot carry out your task,' he said timidly. The King snorted: 'What about you others?' The bear and the ape were not built for such a huge jump – but the cat bowed and in a moment climbed to the balcony, leapt, and landed gracefully on all fours before the throne. All the animals clapped – except the ape.

Next the King read out: 'To my Lord Bear: He must run round in a circle fast enough to catch his own tail.' Everyone smiled at this, for the bear could lumber rather than run; and he had a stump rather than a tail.

'I fear, your Majesty, that I cannot carry out your task,' he mumbled. But neither the stag nor the ape had a tail long enough to catch. Once more it was the clever cat who danced round and round, chasing his tail. The King, the Princess and all the animals of the court laughed until they cried – except the ape, who did not think the cat's games were at all funny. And of course he was not happy when the cat received another prize.

Next the King read out: 'To Mr Cat (for he was not a Lord): He must sing a beautiful sweet song.'

'With pleasure, your Majesty,' purred the cat.

Now, none of the animals had ever heard the cat do anything but mew a little, and talk of course. *We* know that cats sing to each other at night – and sing of love. But this cat had never sung in public before. All the court was delighted by the sweet music he made, especially the beautiful Princess. Everyone, that is, except the ape, who was furious.

The King read out the last paper: 'To my Lord Ape. He must approach the throne and make a deep and graceful bow.' The ape came forward proudly and bowed *so* low that his hands touched the floor. But someone had laid a patch of glue on that very spot. When Lord Ape tried to rise, he could not. He was stuck fast. The King and all his court burst into laughter. The more the ape pulled, the sillier he looked.

'Take him from the court at once. I have never met such rudeness,' shouted the King, who was angry by this time. And while the ape was being unstuck, the cat bowed elegantly and the stag and the bear bobbed up and down to everyone. They were all very careful to keep away from the patch of glue.

But the King had had enough. 'You are all of you clumsy animals – except the cat. You have all of you failed your test – except the cat. I don't want to see any of you again – except the new Lord Cat. He shall be allowed to marry my beautiful daughter, Princess Squisita. From now on the cat is the only animal who may live in our houses – and only a cat may look at a King.'

The ape slouched off, and since then no ape has ever been able to stand upright again.

Traditional British

The Cat and the Mice

Terrible things were happening in the world of mice, for their enemy, the cat, was always on the prowl and no one felt safe. Something had to be done, if only they knew what. At last the mice all gathered together for a meeting. The doors were locked, and every one of the mice began to think and talk about the best way to solve their terrible problem. They needed a weapon against their enemy. Many mice suggested many schemes, but none of them seemed just right.

At last a bright young mouse stood up on his hind paws and gave a wonderful speech. He came up with an idea which was so clever and so simple that none of the older and wiser mice could understand why they hadn't thought of it themselves long ago.

'Ladies and gentlemen, life is now a danger for us all,' he said. 'But I think I have the answer. I would like to suggest that the cat wears a bell round her neck, day and night. Then we shall always know when she is coming, and have time to escape her cruel claws.'

All the other mice clapped their paws when they heard this brilliant suggestion. One of them got up to say: 'We should accept this plan without any more delay, and what's more, I propose a vote of thanks to our young friend himself!' Again everyone agreed.

At last an old mouse, who had said nothing till then, stood up to speak.

'Fellow mice,' he said, 'the plan is certainly very clever, and our brilliant young friend of course deserves a vote of thanks from us all; but first could we – with all respect – ask for a little more detail of the plan? I'm quite sure it will work. But could he explain how the bell gets tied round the cat's neck? And which mouse is going to volunteer to hang the bell on the cat?'

Aesop

The Tale of Johnny Town-mouse

Johnny Town-mouse was born in a cupboard. Timmy Willie was born in a garden. Timmy Willie was a little country mouse who went to town by mistake in a hamper. The gardener sent vegetables to town once a week by carrier; he packed them in a big hamper.

The gardener left the hamper by the garden gate, so that the carrier could pick it up when he passed. Timmy Willie crept in through a hole in the wickerwork, and after eating some peas – Timmy Willie fell fast asleep.

He awoke in a fright, while the hamper was being lifted into the carrier's cart. Then there was a jolting, and a clattering of horse's feet; other packages were thrown in; for miles and miles – jolt – jolt – jolt! and Timmy Willie trembled amongst the jumbled up vegetables.

At last the cart stopped at a house, where the hamper was taken out, carried in, and set down. The cook gave the carrier sixpence; the back door banged, and the cart rumbled away. But there was no quiet; there seemed to be hundreds of carts passing. Dogs barked; boys whistled in the streets; the cook laughed, the parlour maid ran up and down-stairs; and a canary sang like a steam engine.

Timmy Willie, who had lived all his life in a garden, was almost frightened to death. Presently the cook opened the hamper and began to unpack the vegetables. Out sprang the terrified Timmy Willie. Up jumped the cook on a chair, exclaiming, 'A mouse! a mouse! Call the cat! Fetch me the poker, Sarah!' Timmy Willie did not wait for Sarah with the poker; he rushed along the skirting board till he came to a little hole, and in he popped.

He dropped half a foot, and crashed into the middle of a mouse dinner party, breaking three glasses. 'Who in the world is this?' inquired Johnny Town-mouse. But after the first exclamation of surprise he instantly recovered his manners.

With the utmost politeness he introduced Timmy Willie to nine other mice, all with long tails and white neckties. Timmy Willie's own tail was insignificant. Johnny Town-mouse and his friends noticed it; but they were too well bred to make personal remarks; only one of them asked Timmy Willie if he had ever been in a trap?

The dinner was of eight courses; not much of anything, but truly elegant. All the dishes were unknown to Timmy Willie, who would have been a little afraid of tasting them; only he was very hungry, and very anxious to behave with company manners. The continual noise upstairs made him so nervous, that he dropped a plate. 'Never mind, they don't belong to us,' said Johnny.

'Why don't those youngsters come back with the dessert?' It should be explained that two young mice, who were waiting on the others, went skirmishing upstairs to the kitchen between courses. Several times they had come tumbling in, squeaking and laughing; Timmy Willie learnt with horror that they were being chased by the cat. His appetite failed, he felt faint. 'Try some jelly?' said Johnny Town-mouse.

'No? Would you rather go to bed? I will show you a most comfortable sofa pillow.' The sofa pillow had a hole in it. Johnny Town-mouse quite honestly recommended it as the best bed, kept exclusively for visitors. But the sofa smelt of cat. Timmy Willie preferred to spend a miserable night under the fender.

It was just the same next day. An excellent breakfast was provided – for mice accustomed to eat bacon; but Timmy Willie had been reared on roots and salad. Johnny Town-mouse and his friends racketted about under the floors, and came boldly out all over the house in the evening. One particularly loud crash had been caused by Sarah tumbling downstairs with the tea-tray; there were crumbs and sugar and smears of jam to be collected, in spite of the cat.

Timmy Willie longed to be at home in his peaceful nest in a sunny bank. The food disagreed with him; the noise prevented him from sleeping. In a few days he grew so thin that Johnny Town-mouse noticed it, and questioned him. He listened to Timmy Willie's story and inquired about the garden. 'It sounds rather a dull place. What do you do when it rains?'

'When it rains, I sit in my little sandy burrow and shell corn and seeds from my autumn store. I peep out at the throstles and blackbirds on the lawn, and my friend Cock Robin. And when the sun comes out again, you should see my garden and the flowers – roses and pinks and pansies – no noise except the birds and bees, and the lambs in the meadows.'

'There goes that cat again!' exclaimed Johnny Town-mouse. When they had taken refuge in the coal-cellar, he continued the conversation; 'I confess I am a little disappointed; we have endeavoured to entertain you, Timothy William.'

'Oh yes, yes, you have been most kind – but I do feel so ill,' said Timmy Willie.

'It may be that your teeth and digestion are unaccustomed to our food – perhaps it might be wiser for you to return in the hamper.'

'Oh? Oh!' cried Timmy Willie.

'Why of course, for the matter of that we could have sent you back last week,' said Johnny rather huffily – 'did you not know that the hamper goes back empty on Saturdays?'

So Timmy Willie said goodbye to his new friends, and hid in the hamper with a crumb of cake and a withered cabbage leaf; and after much jolting, he was set down safely in his own garden.

Sometimes on Saturdays he went to look at the hamper lying by the gate, but he knew better than to get in again. And nobody got out – though Johnny Town-mouse had half promised a visit.

The winter passed; the sun came out again; Timmy Willie sat by his burrow warming his little fur coat and sniffing the smell of violets and spring grass. He had nearly forgotten his visit to town. When up the sandy path, all spick and span with a brown leather bag, came Johnny Town-mouse!

Timmy Willie received him with open arms. 'You have come at the best of the all the year, we will have herb pudding and sit in the sun.'

'H'm'm! it is a little damp,' said Johnny Town-mouse, who was carrying his tail under his arm, out of the mud. 'What is that fearful noise?' he started violently.

'That?' said Timmy Willie, 'that is only a cow. I will beg a little milk, they are quite harmless, unless they happen to lie down on you. How are all our friends?'

Johnny's account was rather middling. He explained

why he was paying his visit so early in the season; the family had gone to the seaside for Easter; the cook was doing spring cleaning, on board wages, with special instructions to clear out the mice. There were four kittens, and the cat had killed the canary.

'They say we did it; but I know better,' said Johnny Town-mouse. 'Whatever is that fearful racket?'

'That is only the lawnmower. I will fetch some of the grass clippings presently to make your bed. I am sure you had better settle in the country, Johnny.'

'H'm'm – we shall see by Tuesday week; the hamper is stopped while they are at the seaside.'

'I am sure you will never want to live in town again,' said Timmy Willie.

But he did. He went back in the very next hamper of vegetables – he said it was too quiet!!

One place suits one person, another place suits another person. For my part I prefer to live in the country, like Timmy Willie.

Aesop, retold by Beatrix Potter

The Mice Who Ate Iron

There was once a young merchant who lost all the money that his father had left him. The only thing left to him in the world was a pair of iron bars. He decided to go abroad to see if his luck would change, and he asked an old friend to look after his iron bars and keep them safe for him until he came back. At least, if things went wrong again, he would always have these to fall back on!

He got back some years later, still without a penny to his name. 'Oh well,' he thought, 'I'll get some money for the iron. That should keep me from starving for a while.' And round he went to his friend to fetch the bars.

But the friend had also had *his* money problems and had sold the iron himself. But he had thought of a good story. 'Oh, thank goodness you're back!' he said. 'I've been trying to get in touch with you for weeks. I'm afraid something terrible has happened. You know that iron you left with me? Well, I went to the warehouse a week or so ago to check that it was all right, and found

– to my horror – that the mice had been at it. I had no idea mice would do a thing like that, but they must have liked the flavour. I'm afraid they have eaten every scrap.'

Well, the young merchant was not all that silly, and he certainly wasn't born yesterday. He was clever enough to see that it would get him nowhere to call the other man a liar. He could not take him to court because he had nothing in writing, and thrashing him wouldn't get back his iron bars, so he decided to make the best of it. 'Well, that's just my luck! Everything else has gone wrong for me, so I suppose I shouldn't be surprised by this happening. I don't expect I'll starve!'

His friend was so relieved that the merchant seemed to have fallen for his ridiculous story that he felt the least he could do – to prevent him from starving – was to ask him to stay to dinner. He sat him down to as much food and wine as he could take. The merchant was remarkably cheerful, considering what had happened, and chattered happily all evening. 'It's amazing,' said the friend to himself. 'Some people will believe anything! No wonder he never makes any money.'

At the end of the evening the merchant said goodbye and set off home. Outside he met his friend's only son, bribed him with sweets, and kidnapped him.

Next day the merchant met his friend again in the street. 'How are you today?' asked the merchant. 'Is something the matter? You look as if you haven't slept a wink.'

'I'm worried out of my mind,' his friend confessed. 'It's our son. He's been missing since last night and we've no idea what's happened to him. He's only eight!'

'Was he wearing a sort of reddish-brown shirt?'

'Yes, that's right,' said the other eagerly.

'And sandals?'

'Have you seen him? Tell me, for God's sake.'

'Well, if it's the boy I'm thinking of – I hardly know how to tell you this. As I was leaving your place last night, an owl swept down from the sky and carried off a lad in a reddish-brown shirt and sandals. In its beak. I was amazed. I had no idea an owl would do a thing like that. It must have liked his flavour. I couldn't believe my own eyes.'

'You're a liar!' screamed his friend. 'No owl could possibly have carried him off. Do you expect me to believe that? You know where he is. If you don't tell me, I'll...'

'What makes you so sure he couldn't have been kidnapped by an owl? Odder things have happened in this odd town. Why, only yesterday I heard a story about some iron bars that had been eaten by mice. Would you believe it?'

So the merchant was not as silly as he looked, and his friend had to own up. 'All right. I know I asked for that. It was a terrible lie, my story about the mice!' – and he burst into tears.

'Well, my story about the owl wasn't exactly the truth. So perhaps we should both apologize. I could probably get your son back for about the price of two iron bars.'

And so they struck a bargain. But somehow they never felt quite the same way about each other again.

Traditional Indian

The Miller, His Son and Their Donkey

A miller and his son decided that they must sell their donkey at the market. They realized that he was bound to fetch a better price if he arrived there looking fresh and in good condition. So they set off at a gentle pace, one walking on either side of their donkey. They had not gone very far when they met a group of people coming in the other direction.

'Good Lord,' one of them called out, 'some people! Why doesn't one of those idiots ride on the donkey? They're both slogging away on foot, while their animal looks as fresh as a daisy.'

This seemed sound sense. So the miller said to himself: 'Why didn't I think of that?' And helped his son on to the donkey's back.

About a quarter of a mile further on, they met someone else. She called out: 'Good Lord! What are young people coming to? How dare you sit in comfort up there, lazy-bones, while your poor old father drags his sore feet along!'

This seemed sound sense, so the old miller said to himself: 'Why didn't I think of that?' And he made his son climb down, and took his place on the donkey's back. They had not gone very much further, when a third person shouted out to them: 'Good Lord, you lazy old man! You call yourself a father, and let that poor little boy walk his feet into blisters while you sit in comfort. How can you?'

This seemed sound sense, so the miller said to himself: 'Why didn't I think of that?' The last thing he wanted was to be a cruel father. So he leant over and helped his son on to the donkey's back behind him.

They were still some way short of the market town when a fourth person passed them. 'Good Lord,' cried the lady, 'how appalling! That poor creature! Imagine – with those two heavy, lazy brutes on its back. Somebody should report them. It's they who ought to be carrying the donkey!'

This seemed sound sense, so the miller said to himself yet again: 'Why didn't I think of that?' The last thing he wanted was to be cruel to his donkey. Down they both got, and he took the donkey's front legs while his son took the back ones.

And that is how they reached the market, sweating under the weight of their donkey. 'Good Lord,' cried the first townsman they met, 'look at those two! They must be mad. Don't they know the donkey is supposed to carry *them*?'

Aesop, retold by Charles Dodsley

The Donkey, the Ox and the Farmer

There was once a rich farmer, who understood the language of the animals and birds. He had hundreds of cattle. He kept an ox and a donkey in one of his stables. At the end of each day, the ox came back to their stall and found it well swept and watered; the manger filled with the best straw and the best barley; and the donkey lying in luxury (because the farmer did not often ride him).

One day the farmer happened to overhear the ox say to the donkey: 'You are lucky! I am worked to the bone, while you stay here in luxury. You eat the best barley and have everything you need. Our master only rides you once in a while. As for me, my life is slavery, whether I am in the field or at the mill.'

'Well,' said the donkey, 'when you're taken to the field and the yoke is strapped on your neck, pretend to be ill and fall to the ground. Don't get up, even if they beat you; or if you do, collapse again on the spot. When they bring you back and give you your food, don't eat it! Refuse it for a day or two; and that way you'll get time off work.'

Remember that the farmer was there and understood every word.

So when the ploughman brought the ox his food, he ate scarcely any of it. And when the ploughman came the following morning to lead him out into the field, the ox seemed to be far from well. The farmer told the ploughman, 'You had better take the donkey and harness him to pull the plough today!'

So the man harnessed up the donkey instead of the ox, and ploughed with him all day.

When the day's work was done and the donkey came back to the stable, the ox thanked him for his good advice. But the donkey remained silent, and bitterly regretted what he had said.

Next day the ploughman came and harnessed the donkey again and made him work till the evening. When the donkey returned, his neck was rubbed raw and he was hardly able to stand up. The ox again said how grateful he was, and praised his cleverness.

'There's such a thing as being too clever,' thought the donkey. Then he turned to the ox and said, 'I have just heard our master say to his servant: "If the ox does not improve soon, take him to the slaughterhouse and make an end of him." I was so worried about your safety, dear friend, that I thought I must tell you this before it's too late. And peace be with you!'

When he heard the donkey's news the ox thanked him and said, 'I'll be only too happy to get back to work tomorrow.' This time he ate *all* his food, and even licked the manger clean.

The farmer and his wife came to visit the ox, first thing next morning. The ploughman arrived and led out the ox. The animal took one look at his master, lowed, and jumped and frisked like a puppy. The farmer laughed so hard that he toppled over.

Traditional Arabic

The Three Little Pigs

There was once upon a time a pig who lived with her three children in a comfortable, old-fashioned farmyard. The eldest of the little pigs was called Browny, the second Whitey, and the youngest and best-looking, Blacky. Now Browny ·spent most of his time rolling and wallowing in the mud. He was never so happy as on a wet day, when the mud in the farmyard was soft and thick.

Then he would steal away from his mother's side and, finding the muddiest place in the yard, would roll about in it and thoroughly enjoy himself. His mother would shake her head sadly, and say, 'Ah, Browny, some day you will be sorry you didn't obey your old mother.' But no words of advice or warning could cure Browny of his bad habits.

Whitey was a clever little pig, but she was greedy. She was always looking forward to her dinner, and when the farm-girl carried the pails across the yard, Whitey would dance with excitement. As soon as the food was poured into the trough, she jostled Blacky

62

and Browny out of the way in her hurry to get the best bits for herself. Her mother often told her that some day she would suffer for being so greedy.

Blacky was a good, sensible little pig, neither dirty nor greedy. He had dainty ways (for a pig) and his skin was always as smooth and shining as black satin. He was far cleverer than Browny or Whitey. His mother's heart would swell with pride when she heard the farmer's friends say that some day the little black piglet would be a prize pig.

Now the time came when the mother pig called the three little pigs round her and said, 'Dear children, I feel I am growing old and weak and haven't long to live. Before I die I'd like to build a house for each of you. Now Browny, what sort of house would you like?'

'A mud house,' replied Browny, looking longingly at a wet puddle in the corner of the yard.

'And you, Whitey?' said the mother pig in a sad voice, for she was disappointed with Browny's choice.

'A cabbage house,' answered Whitey, her mouth full, for she was grubbing among some potato peelings.

'Foolish, foolish child!' said their mother, sadly. 'And you, Blacky,' turning to her youngest, 'what sort of house shall I order for you?'

'A brick house, please mother; it will be warm in winter, cool in summer, and safe all the year round.'

'You're a sensible little pig,' replied his mother. 'I'll see that the three houses are got ready at once. And now, one last piece of advice. You've heard me talk of our old enemy, the wolf. When he hears I am dead, he is sure to try and carry you off to his den. He is very sly, and no doubt he'll disguise himself and pretend to be a friend. But you must promise me not to let him into your houses, no matter what he says.'

The three little pigs promised, and a short time afterwards the old pig died.

Browny was delighted with his soft mud walls and with the clay door, though soon the house looked like nothing but a big mud pie. One day, as he was lying half asleep in the mud, he heard a soft knock at his door, and an oily voice said: 'May I come in, dear Browny? I want to see your beautiful new house.'

'Who are you?' said Browny, jumping up in a great fright.

'I am a friend come to call on you,' answered the voice.

'No, no,' replied Browny, 'you are the wicked wolf. Mother warned us against you. I won't let you in.'

'Oho! That's not very polite!' said the wolf, speaking roughly in his wolfy voice. 'We'll see about that. I'll huff and I'll puff. And I'll blow your house down!' And he made a large hole in the soft mud walls. In a twinkling he jumped through it, caught Browny by his neck, flung him over his shoulder and trotted off to his den.

The next day, as Whitey was munching a few leaves of cabbage from her house, the wolf stole up to her door. He began speaking in the same oily voice he had used with Browny. She was very frightened when he said: 'I'm a friend who's come to visit you and share some of your crispy cabbage for dinner.'

'Please don't touch it,' cried Whitey in horror. 'The cabbages are the walls of my house. If you eat them you'll make a hole, and the wind and rain will come in and give me a cold. Please go away! I'm sure you're not a friend, but our wicked enemy, the wolf.'

Poor Whitey began to whine and whimper. She wished she had not been such a greedy little pig and had chosen something more solid than cabbages for her walls. But it was too late now.

'I'll huff and I'll puff. And I'll blow your house

down!' roared the wolf. And in a twinkling he forced his way through the walls and carried the trembling, shivering Whitey off to his den.

Next day the wolf started off for Blacky's house. But when he reached the brick house, he found the door bolted and barred. In his oily voice he began: 'Do let me in, dear Blacky. I have brought you a present of some eggs I picked up in a farmyard on my way.'

'No, no, Mr Wolf,' replied Blacky. 'I am not going to open my door to you. I know your cunning ways.'

The wolf was so angry that he dashed against the wall and tried to knock it down. 'I'll huff and I'll puff. And I'll blow your house down!' he snarled. But it was strong and well built.

The wolf scraped and tore at the bricks with his paws, but he only hurt himself. At last he had to give up, and limped away, his paws bleeding and sore. 'Never mind!' he cried, as he went off. 'I'll get you one day soon, see if I don't. And I'll grind your bones to powder when I have you in my den.' And he snarled fiercely and showed his teeth.

Next day Blacky had to go to the town to buy a big kettle. As he was walking home, he heard stealthy footsteps behind him. For a moment his heart stood still. He had just reached the top of a hill and could see his own little house nestling among the trees. In a twinkling he snatched the lid off the kettle and jumped in. Coiling himself round, he lay quite snug in the bottom of the kettle. He managed to slide the lid on so that he was entirely hidden. With a little kick he started the kettle off, and down the hill it went. All the wolf saw was a very large black kettle rolling down at a great speed. But the kettle stopped close to the little brick house, and in a twinkling Blacky jumped out and ran inside. He barred and bolted the door and put the shutters up.

'Oho!' cried the wolf. 'You think you'll escape me

that way, do you? We'll soon see about that, my friend.' And round the house he crept.

Blacky filled the kettle, put it on the fire, and sat down quietly. Just as the water came to the boil he heard a soft, muffled patter, patter, above him. The next moment he saw the wolf's head and front paws coming down the chimney. The wolf slipped and fell with a scream into the boiling water – and that was the end of him.

As soon as he was sure their wicked enemy was dead, Blacky went to rescue Browny and Whitey. He could hear his poor brother and sister crying and squealing in the den. When they saw Blacky they jumped for joy. He soon found a sharp stone and cut them loose. Then all three started off together for Blacky's house, where they lived happily ever after. Browny gave up mud, and Whitey gave up being greedy – for they never forgot that these faults had nearly put an end to them.

Traditional British

The Wind and the Sun

The north wind and the sun were quarrelling. Each of them claimed: 'I am stronger than you!' In the end, they agreed to hold a competition and settle the question once and for all. 'Do you see that man down there, wrapped in a coat? Whichever of us can get that coat off his back is the winner,' suggested the sun. So the wind had first go.

He blew and he blew: first an icy wind, and then an arctic gale. But however hard he blew, the man only wrapped the coat round himself more tightly. Though the gale became a hurricane, the man just humped his coat more snugly than ever round his shoulders, and added another layer to keep himself from freezing. Even the north wind can get out of breath, and he ran out of patience too and gave up.

Next it was the sun's turn. Her warm rays broke through the chill mist the wind had left. As the sun got hotter, first the man unwound his scarf, then he unbuttoned his coat. Before long he took it off altogether. As the sun got stronger and stronger, the man took off more and more of his clothes. In the end he went to cool off in the river.

After that, there could be no doubt which was the stronger of the two.

Aesop

The Case of the Smell

In the far north-west of China there lived Effendi Nasreddin. He was the cleverest man for miles around, and many people came to ask his advice. Once a very poor man came to see him for just this reason. He bowed very low and very humbly, and said: 'I hardly dare to beg you to help someone who is as poor and unworthy as I am. But I have a great favour to ask of you.'

'I shall be delighted if I can be of help to you. So tell me what I can do,' replied the Effendi.

The poor man sighed. 'Life is hard for people as poor as I am. Yesterday I was passing the door of that restaurant owned by Lord Enibi. I paused for a moment because the food smelt so delicious. Lord Enibi himself pounced on me. He said he had caught me swallowing the smell of his food, and handed me a bill! As you can imagine, I hadn't a single penny to pay him. So he dragged me before the Judge. Judge Cadi said he needed to sleep on the case, but he is going to pass sentence today. Could you possibly come along to the court and say something in my defence?'

'Of course I'll come to the court with you,' said the Effendi, 'and see what I can do to help.'

When they reached the court, Lord Enibi and Judge Cadi were already there, talking and laughing together. But as soon as the Judge saw the poor man, he suddenly looked solemn. 'You should be ashamed of yourself,' he shouted angrily. 'You have filled yourself up with the smells from Lord Enibi's restaurant. But you haven't paid him a penny. Pay him what you owe him at once, do you hear!'

The Effendi stepped forward and bowed the deepest of bows. 'It so happens that this poor man is my younger brother. He hasn't a penny, so I've come along to settle his debt.'

Then he took a bulging purse that hung on his belt. He held it up to Lord Enibi's ear and shook it till all the coins jingled inside. 'Can you hear the money rattling then, my lord?' said the Effendi cheerfully.

'Don't be silly! I'm not deaf. Of course I can hear it,' replied Lord Enibi crossly.

'Excellent. I'm so glad that is settled. The debt is cancelled, of course. My brother smelled your food cooking, and now you have heard his money jingling. So that puts things straight between you.'

And with that, Effendi Nasreddin turned on his heel and gave the poor man his arm. Together they walked out of the court.

Traditional Chinese

The Wonderful Tar-baby

One day Brer Fox went to work, got some tar, mixed in some turpentine and fixed up a contraption (like a sticky scarecrow) called a Tar-baby. He took this Tar-baby and set her up by the road, and then he slunk off into the bushes to see what would happen. He didn't have to wait long either, because by-and-by Brer Rabbit came jogging down the road – lippity-clippity, clippity-lippity, just as saucy as a jay. Brer Fox, he lay low. Brer Rabbit came prancing along until he spied the Tar-baby, and then he stood back on his hind legs as though he was astonished. Tar-baby she sat there, she did, and Brer Fox he lay low.

'Morning!' says Brer Rabbit. 'Nice weather this morning,' says he. Tar-baby she ain't saying nothing and Brer Fox, he lay low. 'How are you feeling, this fine day?' asks Brer Rabbit.

Brer Fox winked his eye slowly and lay low, and Tar-baby, she ain't saying nothing.

'How you coming on then? Are you deaf?' says Brer

71

Rabbit. 'Because if you are, I can holler louder,' he says. Tar-baby stayed still, and Brer Fox, he lay low.

'You're stuck-up, that's what you are,' says Brer Rabbit. 'And I'm going to cure you, that's what I'm-a-going to do.' Brer Fox sort of chuckled in his stomach, he did, but Tar-baby ain't saying nothing.

'I'm going to teach you how to talk to respectable folk if it's the last thing I do,' says Brer Rabbit. 'If you don't take off that hat and say howdy-do to me, I'm going to bust you wide open,' says he. Tar-baby stayed still, and Brer Fox, he lay low.

Brer Rabbit keeps on asking, and Tar-baby keeps on saying nothing. In the end, Brer Rabbit drew back his fist and – blip – he struck her on the side of the head. His fist stuck and he couldn't pull it away. Tar-baby held him. But Tar-baby stayed still, and Brer Fox, he lay low.

'If you don't let go of me, I'll hit you again,' says Brer Rabbit. He fetched her a swipe with his other hand, and that stuck. Tar-baby ain't saying nothing, and Brer Fox, he lay low.

'Turn me loose, before I kick the natural stuffing out of you,' says Brer Rabbit, but Tar-baby ain't saying nothing. She just held on and Brer Rabbit lost the use of his feet in the same way. Brer Fox, he lay low.

Then Brer Rabbit yells out that if Tar-baby didn't let him go, he'd butt her crank-sided. And butt her he did – and his head got stuck. Then out sauntered Brer Fox, looking as innocent as a mocking-bird.

'Howdy, Brer Rabbit,' says Brer Fox. 'You look sort of stuck up this morning.' Then he rolled on the ground and laughed and laughed till he could laugh no more.

By and by he ups and says: 'Well, I expect I've got you this time, Brer Rabbit,' says he. 'Maybe I ain't, but I expect I have. You've been running round here sassying after me for a mighty long time, but I expect you've come to the end of the row. You've been bouncing round in this neighbourhood until you've come to believe you're the boss of the whole gang. And then you're always somewhere you've no business to be, Brer Rabbit. Who asked you to come and strike up an acquaintance with this here Tar-baby? And who stuck you up there where you are? Nobody in the round world. You just stuck and jammed yourself on that Tar-baby without waiting for any invite,' says Brer Fox, says he. 'And there you are, and there you'll stay till I fix up a brush-pile and fire her up. Because I'm going to barbecue you this day, for sure,' says Brer Fox, says he.

Then Brer Rabbit talked mighty humble. 'I don't care what you do with me, Brer Fox,' says he, 'so long as you don't fling me into that briar-patch. Roast me, Brer Fox,' says he, 'but don't fling me into that briar-patch.'

'I ain't got no string,' says Brer Fox, 'and now I expect I'll have to drown you.'

'Drown me just as deep as you please, Brer Fox,' says Brer Rabbit, 'but don't fling me into that briar-patch.'

'There ain't no water near,' says Brer Fox, says he, 'and now I expect I'll have to skin you.'

'Skin me, Brer Fox,' says Brer Rabbit. 'Snatch out my eyeballs, tear out my ears by the roots, and cut off my legs,' says he, 'but please, Brer Fox, don't fling me into that briar-patch.'

Because Brer Fox wanted to hurt Brer Rabbit as badly as he could, he caught him by the hind legs and slung him right into the middle of the briar-patch. There was a considerable flutter as Brer Rabbit struck the bushes and Brer Fox sort of hung around to see what was going to happen. By-and-by he heard someone calling to him and way up the hill he saw Brer Rabbit sitting cross-legged on a chinkapin log, combing the tar out of his hair with a chip. Then Brer Fox knew he had been tricked mighty badly. Brer Rabbit was pleased to fling back some of his sauce, and he hollers out: 'Bred and born in a briar-patch, Brer Fox – bred and born in a briar-patch!' And with that he skipped away just as lively as a cricket in the embers.

From Uncle Remus *by Joel Chandler Harris*

The Lion and the Rabbit

Deep in the jungle lived a huge lion. All the other animals were afraid of him because so many of them had been killed and eaten by him. And they felt that there would soon be no one left. After a long debate, they decided they must go and talk to the lion himself. A group was chosen and they all trooped off to the lion's den.

He was very glad to see so many fine future meals appear on his doorstep, without him having to make any effort. But he roared fiercely: 'What do you lot want?'

'Your Royal Highness,' said the fox humbly – for he had been chosen to speak for the others, 'with all respect, we are worried. You kill so many of us every day. We, your loyal subjects, fear that soon there won't be enough of us left to give you regular healthy meals. You could become a king with no subjects left – and a king-sized hunger!'

The lion did not look at all keen at this prospect.

'So, your Majesty,' the fox went on smoothly, 'we

have a plan to make sure that you are comfortable and fully fed for ever. You won't have to waste your noble energy hunting, for we will send you an animal every day. That way there'll be less worry for all of us.'

The lion was very greedy and very lazy, but not very clever. He thought for a long time, in case this was some trick, but at last – as though he were doing everyone a great favour – he said: 'All right, I'm prepared to try it. But if you miss a single day, watch out, because I'll come and kill as many of you as I fancy.'

'Of course,' they agreed. 'But leave it to us. We'll give you first-class service.'

From then onwards, an animal was sent every day to the lion, and the lion kept his side of the bargain. Each type of animal took its turn, until at last it was the rabbit's. A clever old rabbit was chosen. But, since he was in no particular hurry to be the lion's supper, he walked slowly through the jungle. He rested from time to time, but kept thinking all the way. He only ran the last few yards, and by that time he was very late.

The lion was angry at being kept waiting so long for his supper, but he was *furious* when he saw a snack rather than a proper meal in front of him. 'You are disgustingly late! You are disgustingly small! Who on earth sent you? This service just isn't good enough. They're not keeping their side of the bargain, so I don't see why I should keep mine,' he roared.

The rabbit bowed very low and replied: 'Your Majesty. Please don't blame me or any of the other animals for what has gone wrong today. Of course we all know that a little rabbit is not a meal fit for a king. Six of us set out, keen for the honour of serving you. But I'm afraid my five brothers were caught and eaten on the way here – by another lion – your Majesty, sir!'

'Another lion?' bellowed the King. 'Where did you see him? Who was he?'

76

'Well, he was enormous,' said the rabbit, rolling his eyes wildly. 'He came out of a hole in the ground, and he wanted to kill me too. But I warned him. I told him we had the honour to be your Majesty's supper – and that six was barely enough for your royal appetite, never mind *one!* – that you would be *furious!* – and that you wouldn't take that sort of treatment lying down. Then the lion asked who you were. I told him: "He is our king, of course, the biggest lion in the jungle." Then – I hardly dare tell you what this other lion replied, your Majesty. He roared: "*I* am the biggest lion in the jungle. *I* am your king. This other lion must be a cheat. Just you bring him along and I'll show him who's boss. You tell him that from me."

The king lion had gone from angry to furious as the rabbit told this story. By the end he couldn't bottle up his fury a moment longer. He thundered: 'Lead me to him!' and all the trees in the jungle shook. 'Take me there at once, and I'll tear him limb from limb!'

'Oh, thank goodness, your Majesty. That's just what I longed to do myself – only of course I'm far too small. Follow me, sir.'

The rabbit led the lion to a well in the jungle. 'Here we are, your Majesty. He lives down there,' whispered the rabbit, and he pointed down the well.

'Leave him to me!' raged the lion. 'Where are you?'

'Oh, do be careful, sir – he must be down there in his den!'

'Just you show me!'

The rabbit led the lion to the edge of the well and told him to look down. The lion saw his own reflection staring back at him from the water.

The king lion roared his challenge. His own roar echoed back from the well. But the lion thought it was the roar of his enemy. He exploded again, with an even louder roar. Back came the echo, louder still.

This was too much for the king lion. In a frenzy he

jumped into the well to kill his enemy – down and
down he fell, to the very bottom. He landed with an
almighty crash and was killed.

The rabbit went home happily, to tell all the other
animals that now they could live in safety.

Traditional Indian

One Swallow Doesn't Make a Summer

There was once a young man who had been left a great deal of money, but he lost every penny of it. In the end he was left with nothing but the clothes he stood up in, including a warm cloak. Through the winter this covered him by day, and became a blanket at night. When the young man was wondering desperately what he would do next, he caught sight of a swallow skimming through the air. It had flown back earlier than usual from abroad. The young man welcomed it like a long-lost friend.

'If the swallows are back, that must mean summer is here. Thank goodness! I shall get by all right after all. Now I can sell my cloak, for I shan't need it again.' So that is just what he did. He sold it, like everything else.

But the very next day, the weather was freezing and there was a stiff frost that night. Winter wasn't over, after all.

Next morning the young man felt chilled to the

bone. The first thing he saw was the body of the poor swallow, which had frozen to death.

'Oh, you miserable bird,' said the young man. 'You have been the death of yourself, and were almost the death of me.'

Aesop

How the Polar Bear Became

When the animals had been on earth for some time they grew tired of admiring the trees, the flowers, and the sun. They began to admire each other. Every animal was eager to be admired, and spent a part of each day making itself look more beautiful.

Soon they began to hold beauty contests.

Sometimes Tiger won the prize, sometimes Eagle, and sometimes Ladybird. Every animal tried hard.

One animal in particular won the prize almost every time. This was Polar Bear.

Polar Bear was white. Not quite snowy white, but much whiter than any of the other creatures. Everyone admired her. In secret, too, everyone was envious of her. But however much they wished that she wasn't quite so beautiful, they couldn't help giving her the prize.

'Polar Bear,' they said, 'with your white fur, you are almost too beautiful.'

All this went to Polar Bear's head. In fact, she became vain. She was always washing and polishing her fur, trying to make it still whiter. After a while she was winning the prize every time. The only times any other creature got a chance to win was when it rained. On those days Polar Bear would say:

'I shall not go out in the wet. The other creatures will be muddy, and my white fur may get splashed.'

Then, perhaps, Frog or Duck would win for a change.

She had a crowd of young admirers who were always hanging around her cave. They were mainly Seals, all very giddy. Whenever she came out they made a loud shrieking roar:

'Oooooooh! How beautiful she is!'

Before long, her white fur was more important to Polar Bear than anything. Whenever a single speck of dust landed on the tip of one hair of it – she was furious.

'How can I be expected to keep beautiful in this country!' she cried then. 'None of you have ever seen me at my best, because of the dirt here. I am really much whiter than any of you have ever seen me. I think I shall have to go into another country. A country where there is none of this dust. Which country would be best?'

She used to talk in this way because then the Seals would cry:

'Oh, please don't leave us. Please don't take your beauty away from us. We will do anything for you.'

And she loved to hear this.

Soon animals were coming from all over the world to look at her. They stared and stared as Polar Bear stretched out on her rock in the sun. Then they went off home and tried to make themselves look like her. But it was no use. They were all the wrong colour. They were black, or brown, or yellow, or ginger, or fawn or speckled, but not one of them was white. Soon most of them gave up trying to look beautiful.

But they still came every day to gaze enviously at Polar Bear. Some brought picnics. They sat in a vast crowd among the trees in front of her cave.

'Just look at her,' said Mother Hippo to her children. 'Now see that you grow up like that.'

But nothing pleased Polar Bear.

'The dust these crowds raise!' she sighed. 'Why can't I ever get away from them? If only there were some spotless, shining country, all for me...'

Now pretty well all the creatures were tired of her being so much more admired than they were. But one creature more so than the rest. He was Peregrine Falcon.

He was a beautiful bird, all right. But he was not white. Time and again, in the beauty contest he was runner-up to Polar Bear.

'If it were not for her,' he raged to himself, 'I should be first every time.'

He thought and thought for a plan to get rid of her. How? How? How? At last he had it.

One day he went up to Polar Bear.

Now Peregrine Falcon had been to every country in the world. He was a great traveller, as all the creatures well knew.

'I know a country,' he said to Polar Bear, 'which is so clean it is even whiter than you are. Yes, yes, I know, you are beautifully white, but this country is even whiter. The rocks are clean glass and the earth is frozen ice-cream. There is no dirt there, no dust, no mud. You would become whiter than ever in that country. And no one lives there. You could be queen of it.'

Polar Bear tried to hide her excitement.

'I could be queen of it, you say?' she cried. 'This country sounds made for me. No crowds, no dirt? And the rocks, you say, are glass?'

'The rocks,' said Peregrine Falcon, 'are mirrors.'

'Wonderful!' cried Polar Bear.

'And the rain,' he said, 'is white face powder.'

'Better than ever!' she cried. 'How quickly can I be there, away from all these staring crowds and all this dirt?'

'I am going to another country,' she told the other animals. 'It is too dirty here to live.'

Peregrine Falcon hired Whale to carry his passenger. He sat on Whale's forehead, calling out the directions. Polar Bear sat on the shoulder, gazing at the sea. The Seals, who had begged to go with her, sat on the tail.

After some days, they came to the North Pole, where it is all snow and ice.

'Here you are,' cried Peregrine Falcon. 'Everything just as I said. No crowds, no dirt, nothing but beautiful clean whiteness.'

'And the rocks actually are mirrors!' cried Polar Bear, and she ran to the nearest iceberg to repair her beauty after the long trip.

Every day now, she sat on one iceberg or another, making herself beautiful in the mirror of the ice. Always, near her, sat the Seals. Her fur became whiter and whiter in this new clean country. And as it became whiter, the Seals praised her beauty more and more. When she herself saw the improvement in her looks she said:

'I shall never go back to that dirty old country again.'

And there she is still, with all her admirers around her.

Peregrine Falcon flew back to the other creatures and told them that Polar Bear had gone for ever. They were all very glad, and set about making themselves beautiful at once. Every single one was saying to himself:

'Now that Polar Bear is out of the way, perhaps I shall have a chance of the prize at the beauty contest.'

And Peregrine Falcon was saying to himself:

'Surely, now, I am the most beautiful of all creatures.'

But that first contest was won by Little Brown Mouse for her pink feet.

Ted Hughes

The Two Friends

Two friends were walking along together and talking, when all of a sudden a bear appeared. Quick as a flash, one of them ran across to a tree, climbed it, and hid among the leaves. The other looked around helplessly for somewhere else to hide – then, when the bear was almost on top of him, he fell flat on the ground. The bear sniffed him all over. The poor man lay still as a stone and pretended to be dead. He remembered someone telling him that bears won't touch a corpse.

In the end the bear turned and went back into the forest, leaving the man alive but terrified. His friend climbed down from his tree and walked over to him. 'What on earth did that bear whisper in your ear?' he asked.

'Oh, he was a wise old bear and he gave me some very sensible advice: "Don't go around in future with anyone who runs away at the first sign of danger. A friend in need is a friend indeed." How right he was!'

Aesop

The Bear and the Fox

One day, while Osmo the bear was hunting in the forest, he caught a grouse.

'Not bad,' he said to himself. 'All the other animals would be impressed if they could see what I've caught.' Osmo wasn't the swiftest and quietest hunter in the world, you see.

He was so pleased with himself that he was desperate to show someone what he had done. Holding the bird carefully between his teeth so as not to harm it, he trundled off down the forest path in search of some other animal.

'I can't wait to see the expression on their faces when they see this plump grouse,' he thought. 'They won't be able to call me an awkward idiot any more.'

Mikko, the fox, was the first animal he met. Mikko immediately saw how pleased Osmo was with himself, but wasn't going to give the old bear any satisfaction. He looked casually up at Osmo, completely ignored the grouse, and said: 'Oh, it's you, Osmo. I hardly noticed you.' Then he sniffed the air.

Osmo grunted frantically, to catch the fox's attention. 'Mmh! Mmh!'

'Osmo, which direction is the wind coming from? I can't make up my mind,' said Mikko.

'Mmh! Mmh!' grunted Osmo, and rolled his eyes, still trying to draw the fox's attention to his prize.

Mikko still refused to look at Osmo, or the grouse. He sniffed again. 'I reckon it's a south wind, you know. It is, isn't it, Osmo?'

The bear could only continue to grunt, 'Mmh! Mmh!' – for of course he didn't dare to open his mouth.

'Are you sure it's from the south, Osmo?'

Osmo's grunts were getting angrier and angrier!

'Oh, it's not a south wind. Then what direction do you reckon it *is* coming from?'

Osmo could stand it no longer. He roared: 'North!' And as he opened his mouth to roar, the grouse flew off.

'Now look what you've done!' bellowed the bear. 'You've made me lose my lovely fat grouse. It was all your fault!'

'*I* made you? I don't understand. How on earth was it *my* fault?'

'You kept asking me about the wind. So of course I *had* to open my mouth. And now look what has happened!'

'Too bad! But why *did* you open your mouth?'

'Well, you can't say "North" if you don't, can you?'

Mikko laughed. 'Look, don't blame me, blame yourself. If I'd been in your place, with a bird in *my* mouth, you wouldn't catch me saying "North".'

'What would *you* have said, then?'

Mikko laughed again. Then he clenched his teeth and mumbled, 'East!'

Traditional Finnish

How the Rhinoceros Got his Skin

Once upon a time, on an uninhabited island on the shores of the Red Sea, there lived a Parsee from whose hat the rays of the sun were reflected in more-than-oriental splendour. And the Parsee lived by the Red Sea with nothing but his hat and his knife and a cooking-stove of the kind that you must particularly never touch. And one day he took flour and water and currants and plums and sugar and things, and made himself one cake which was two feet across and three feet thick. It was indeed a Superior Comestible (*that's* Magic), and he put it on the stove because *he* was allowed to cook on that stove, and he baked it and he baked it till it was all done brown and smelt most sentimental. But just as he was going to eat it there came down to the beach from the Altogether Un-inhabited Interior one Rhinoceros with a horn on his nose, two piggy eyes, and few manners. In those days the Rhinoceros's skin fitted him quite tight. There were no wrinkles in it anywhere. He looked exactly like a Noah's Ark Rhinoceros, but of course much bigger. All the same, he had no manners then, and he has no manners now, and he never will have any manners. He said, 'How!' and the Parsee left that cake and climbed to the top of a palm-tree with nothing on but his hat, from which the rays of the sun were always reflected in more-than-oriental splendour. And the Rhinoceros upset the oil-stove with his nose, and the cake rolled on the sand, and he spiked that cake on the horn of his nose, and he ate it, and he went away, waving his tail, to the desolate and Exclusively Uninhabited Interior which abuts on the islands of Mazanderan, Socotra, and the Promontories of the larger Equinox. Then the Parsee came down from his palm-tree and put the stove on its legs and recited the following *Sloka*, which, as you have not heard, I will now proceed to relate:

> Them that takes cakes
> Which the Parsee-man bakes
> Makes dreadful mistakes.

And there was a great deal more in that than you would think.

Because, five weeks later, there was a heatwave in the Red Sea, and everybody took off all the clothes they had. The Parsee took off his hat; but the Rhinoceros took off his skin and carried it over his shoulder as he came down to the beach to bathe. In those days it buttoned underneath with three buttons and looked like a waterproof. He said nothing whatever about the Parsee's cake, because he had eaten it all; and he never had any manners, then, since, or henceforward. He waddled straight into the water and blew bubbles through his nose, leaving his skin on the beach.

Presently the Parsee came by and found the skin, and

he smiled one smile that ran all round his face two times. Then he danced three times round the skin and rubbed his hands. Then he went to his camp and filled his hat with cake-crumbs, for the Parsee never ate anything but cake, and never swept out his camp. He took that skin, and he shook that skin, and he scrubbed that skin, and he rubbed that skin just as full of old, dry, stale, tickly cake-crumbs and some burned currants as ever it could *possibly* hold. Then he climbed to the top of his palm-tree and waited for the Rhinoceros to come out of the water and put it on.

And the Rhinoceros did. He buttoned it up with the three buttons, and it tickled like cake-crumbs in bed. Then he wanted to scratch, but that made it worse; and then he lay down on the sands and rolled and rolled and rolled, and every time he rolled the cake-crumbs tickled him worse and worse and worse. Then he ran to the palm-tree and rubbed and rubbed and rubbed himself against it. He rubbed so much and so hard that he rubbed his skin into a great fold over his shoulders, and another fold underneath, where the buttons used to be (but he rubbed the buttons off), and he rubbed some more folds over his legs. And it spoiled his temper, but it didn't make the least difference to the cake-crumbs. They were inside his skin and they tickled. So he went home, very angry indeed and horribly scratchy; and from that day to this, every rhinoceros has great folds in his skin and a very bad temper, all on account of the cake-crumbs inside.

But the Parsee came down from his palm-tree, wearing his hat, from which the rays of the sun were reflected in more-than-oriental splendour, packed up his cooking-stove, and went away in the direction of Orotavo, Amygdala, the Upland Meadows of Antananarivo, and the Marshes of Sonaput.

Rudyard Kipling

The Monkey and the Spectacles

Once upon a time, there was a monkey who was growing old. And as he got older, his eyesight got worse and worse. But he had often eavesdropped and heard human beings talking to each other. They did not seem to worry when they got old and could see less clearly. They said: 'I need glasses.'

So the monkey set about getting himself glasses. He collected a pair of spectacles from here and another pair from there, until he had six different pairs.

'That should be enough to help me to see better,' he said confidently.

There was only one snag. Once he had got the spectacles he had no idea what to do with them. He tried everything. He hung them up in every way he could think of. He tried carrying them on his tail. He tried carrying them on his head. He tried sniffing them. He experimented with licking them every night and again every morning. He thought of stirring them into water. But none of these seemed to make him see any better at all.

'Good gracious,' he said in the end, 'I was silly to listen to anything these humans say. It must have been some sort of a joke. I ought to have learned by now! Never believe a word they say.' And one by one he threw the pairs of spectacles away. They were all smashed to pieces on the rocks below – but of course the silly monkey could not see that because he was far too short-sighted!

Traditional Russian, retold by Ivan Krilov

The Baboon and the Tortoise

One day the baboon and the tortoise made a pact of friendship. They both decided to marry, and to invite each other to their weddings. When the baboon celebrated his wedding the tortoise arrived, but he was told by the baboon to come and sit on the tree, 'Because that is good manners in the country of the baboons. It is very rude to eat while lying on the floor,' said the baboon sternly. Of course the tortoise could not remain seated for a long time, because whenever he wanted to reach for the food he fell flat on his belly and all the baboons laughed. They ate all the delicious food and the tortoise got very little. But in the end he got his revenge, because baboons have to walk on all fours.

When it was time for the tortoise to marry, he of course invited the baboon to his party. 'But,' he told him, 'remember that you must come with clean hands, for you know very well it is an offence to arrive at a dinner-party with dirty hands.' Before the baboon arrived, the tortoise burnt the dry grass round his house and all the scrub as well. When the baboon arrived, having carefully washed his hands, he had to walk through the charred grass and so his hands and feet were dirty again. The tortoise sent him back saying: 'Did I not tell you to come with clean hands? Go back to the river and wash your hands.' When the baboon came back, having washed his hands again, he had to walk through the same charred grass and sooty dust. The tortoise sent him back a second time, and a third, until all the splendid dishes had been eaten by the tortoise and his relatives. *Tortoises are wiser because they live longer.*

Traditional Swahili, retold by Jan Knappert

Brer Rabbit Finds His Match at Last

One day, when Brer Rabbit was going lippity-clippiting down the road, he met up with old Brer Terrapin, and after they had passed the time of day with one another they started talking. They kept on talking, they did, till by-and-by they got to disputing which one of them was the faster. Brer Rabbit he said he could outrun Brer Terrapin – and Brer Terrapin he swore he could outrun Brer Rabbit. On and on they argued, till the next thing you know, Brer Terrapin said he'd got a fifty-dollar bill in the chink of the chimney at home, and that money told him he could beat Brer Rabbit in a fair race. Then Brer Rabbit said he'd got a fifty-dollar bill which told him that he could leave Brer Terrapin so far behind, that he could sow barley as he went along and it would be ripe enough to cut by the time Brer Terrapin passed that way.

Anyhow, they laid their bets and put up the money. Old Brer Turkey Buzzard was asked to be judge and to hold the bets. It wasn't long before all the arrangements were made. The race was over five miles. The course was measured out, and a post was set up at every mile along it. Brer Rabbit was to run down the road, and Brer Terrapin said he'd gallop through the woods. Folks told him he could get along faster on the road, but old Brer Terrapin he knew what he was doing. Brer Rabbit trained every day, and skimmed over the ground as gaily as a cricket in June. Old Brer Terrapin, he laid low in the swamp.

Brer Terrapin had a wife and three children, and they were all the very spitting image of the old man. You'd need a spy-glass to tell one from another – and even then you'd be more than likely to make a mistake.

That's the way matters stood until the day of the race – and that morning old Brer Terrapin and his wife and their three children were up before dawn and went to the race-track. The old woman placed herself near the first mile-post, and the children near the others, up to the very last one where old Brer Terrapin took up position himself. By-and-by other people arrived. Judge Buzzard came, and finally Brer Rabbit appeared with ribbons tied round his neck and streaming from his ears. The folks all went along to the finishing-post to see who would be the winner.

When the time came, Judge Buzzard strutted round, pulled out his watch, and hollered: 'Gents, are you ready?'

Brer Rabbit, he said 'Yes,' and old Mrs Terrapin hollered, 'Go!' from the edge of the wood. Brer Rabbit set out on the race and old Mrs Terrapin set out for home. Judge Buzzard rose in the air and skimmed along to see the race was run fairly. When Brer Rabbit got to the first mile-post, one of the terrapin children crawled out of the woods and made for the place. Brer Rabbit, he hollered out: 'Where are you, Brer Terrapin?'

'Here I come a-bulging,' said the terrapin, said he.

Brer Rabbit was so glad he was ahead that he put out harder than ever, while the terrapin made for home. When he came to the next mile-post, another terrapin crawled out of the woods.

'Where are you, Brer Terrapin?' cried Brer Rabbit, said he.

'Here I come a-boiling,' said the terrapin, said he.

Brer Rabbit ran on, and when he came to the next mile-post, there was the terrapin. When he had only one more mile to run, he began to feel out of breath. By-and-by, old Brer Terrapin looked way off down the road. He saw Judge Buzzard sailing along, and knew it was time for him to be up. So he scrambled out of the woods, rolled across the ditch, shuffled through the crowd, reached the mile-post and crawled behind it.

By-and-by, the next thing you know, there was Brer Rabbit. He looked round, and not seeing Brer Terrapin, bawled out: 'Give me the money, Brer Buzzard, give me the money!'

Then old Brer Terrapin, he rose up from behind the post and said, said he: 'If you'll just give me time to catch my breath, ladies and gents, one and all, I expect to get my hands on that money myself.' And sure enough, Brer Terrapin tied the purse round his neck and skedaddled off home.

From Uncle Remus *by Joel Chandler Harris*

The Turtle and the Geese

Beside a spacious lake there lived a turtle and two geese. One summer, however, the country was struck by a drought so fierce that the lake dried up. The waters where the three friends had swum and had dived for their food became dry, cracked mud.

The geese decided that they must leave and search for a new home. So they went sadly to say farewell to their old friend the turtle.

'It hurts us to desert you and the lake where we have been so happy together, but there's nothing else for it,' they explained.

'It's all very well for creatures like you who can fly,' said the turtle bitterly. 'But what about me? You may love the water, but at least you can get your food in other ways. But I can't live out of it. My friends, how can you abandon me to this slow death?' On and on he went, for turtles are great talkers, of course.

'If only we could help! But you don't have wings,' answered the gander. 'We'll certainly put our heads together, though, and see if we can come up with something.' The geese then went into a goosey huddle. 'Things *can* fly, can't they, even if they don't have wings; kites, for instance? What if...?'

They came back to their friend the turtle. 'Look, we have thought of a way of doing it. We'll show you what we mean.'

They soon returned with a long stick. They explained their plan very tactfully: 'This is what you have to do, friend turtle – grip the stick in your mouth. Then we will each take one end of it in our beaks and fly away to a new lake. So we can carry you between us. But, of course, we'll all have to be very careful. No one must say a word on the journey. We must keep *all* our mouths tight shut on the stick, whatever happens.' And they fixed the turtle with a beady eye.

'If you mean me, what *do* you take me for? I'd be a fool to open my mouth when my best friends are saving my life. Let's be off!'

The geese flapped their powerful wings and were soon in the air, heading north to the land of lakes, with the turtle hanging on like grim death between them. All went well until their path lay over a town. Several people looked up and saw the strange procession in the sky. Soon a small crowd gathered. 'What on earth is that? What are those two geese carrying on a stick? I can't believe my eyes! Is it a parcel? Or their nest? No, it's ... a flying turtle!'

The turtle heard all this. He got crosser and crosser, for he didn't like being laughed at or mistaken for a parcel. Instead of biting back his words, he exploded: 'Shut up, you silly gawping humans! Or I'll...'

But he never finished. Down he plunged to the ground, and his shell was shattered into a thousand pieces. And those rude townspeople were rewarded with turtle soup!

Traditional Indian

The Nut and the Church Tower

One day a crow carried a nut off in its beak. But she dropped it into a crack between the stones of a church tower.

'Oh, huge tall tower, have pity on me,' begged the nut humbly. 'I know from the beautiful voice of your bells, as they ring out, that you must be kindly – and that you will help me. When I was ripe, I should have fallen through the branches and landed in the soft rich earth; there I would have been safe, wrapped in dead leaves under my father, the tree. But that cruel crow snatched me away. Now all I long for is to end my life in a small dark hole. May I shelter here among your stones?'

The tower was indeed kind-hearted, and happy to let the nut stay where it had fallen. But it was not long before the little nut split open. Soon it stuck its roots between the stones, and pushed its shoots towards the light. In a few years, the small guest became a big tree that rose high above the church tower. A mass of thick twisting roots split the stones apart.

Then the wall realized it had been stupid to allow the nut to stay. But it was too late. As the years passed the church tower cracked and fell – and a huge nut tree grew out of the ruined wall.

Leonardo da Vinci

The Two Frogs

Once upon a time in the country of Japan there were two frogs, one of whom made his home in a ditch near the town of Osaka, on the sea coast, while the other lived in a clear little stream which ran through the city of Kyoto. At such a great distance apart, they had never even heard of each other; but, oddly enough, both of them thought, at just the same time, that they would like to see a little of the world – the frog who lived in Kyoto wanted to visit Osaka, and the frog who lived in Osaka wished to go to Kyoto where the great Emperor had his palace.

So one fine morning in spring, they both set out along the road that joined Kyoto and Osaka – one from one end and one from the other. The journey was more tiring than they expected, for they did not know much about travelling, or that half-way between the two towns stood a mountain which they would have to climb. It took them a great many hours and a great many hops to reach the top. When each arrived at the summit, imagine his surprise at seeing another frog there!

103

They looked at each other for a moment without speaking, and then fell into conversation, explaining how they came to be so far from home. They were delighted to find that they had both had the same idea – to learn a little more about Japan. As they were not in any hurry, they stretched themselves out in a cool, damp place and agreed that they would have a good rest.

'What a pity we're not taller,' said the Osaka frog, 'for if we could see both towns from here, we could tell if it's worth while going on.'

'We have only to stand up on our hind legs and hold on to each other, and then each of us can see the town he is travelling towards,' replied the Kyoto frog.

The Osaka frog liked this idea. So there they both stood, stretching themselves as high as they could, and holding on to each other tightly so as not to fall over. The Kyoto frog faced Osaka – and the Osaka frog faced Kyoto. But the foolish things forgot that when they stood up their great eyes lay in the backs of their heads. Though their faces were turned towards the cities they wanted to visit, their eyes were fixed on their home towns.

'Dear me,' cried the Osaka frog, 'how disappointing! Kyoto is exactly like Osaka. It's certainly not worth such a long journey. I shall go home!'

'If I'd had any idea that Osaka was only a copy of Kyoto, I would never have travelled all this way!' exclaimed his friend. And as he spoke, he took his legs from his friend's shoulders, and they both fell back on the grass.

Then they said goodbye politely and set off for home again – and to the end of their lives they both believed that Osaka and Kyoto, which look as different as two towns can, were as like as two peas.

Traditional Japanese

The Frog and the Ox

Two young frogs were playing together in a squelchy meadow near their pond. An ox lumbered across this field on his way to the water. He crushed one of the poor frogs with his hoof, and the brother frog hopped off in terror to tell their mother the sad news.

'Tell me what happened. I want every detail,' cried Mother Frog as her son breathlessly told her the story.

'A big rumbling animal. It had four legs and it trampled him into the mud,' sobbed the young frog.

'Big?'

'Yes, Mother, big. Very big.'

'Was it as big as I am?' she asked fiercely.

'Oh yes, much bigger.'

'Bigger than this?' puffed his mother, beginning to blow herself up like a balloon – which is something very clever that frogs can do.

'Oh, far huger. It was huge, Mother.'

'Huger than I am now?' – and she gave herself another puff.

'Oh, far huger. It was an enormous animal.'

Mother Frog did not like the sound of that at all, and

pumped herself still more. 'More enormous than I am now?' She was running out of breath and patience.

'Oh yes, Mother, far more enormous. It was a gigantic animal. You could never get anything like so big, however hard you tried.'

But Mother Frog did not like to be beaten. 'We'll see about that!' she managed to whisper. For she was putting every ounce of breath into blowing herself up. And that is exactly what she did. She blew herself up, and exploded just like a balloon.

Aesop

Moving Day

Turtle forced his eyes open and thrust his head slowly out from his shell to see whether the night had been cold enough to rim his pond with frost. The earth, he found, was still untouched. The sun was late and weak, however, and the brook murmured drowsily as it tumbled over the last bed of rock before reaching the pond. It was time to be thinking about his long winter's sleep.

Suddenly he was no longer content with his way of life. Why did he have to crawl into the mud each autumn and stay there till spring, locked in a silent prison? Why couldn't he have a winter home as nice as some of his friends?

There was Squirrel, for example. What a wonderful nest he had high in the butternut tree! Inside its leafy walls he was safe and comfortable, with enough room to move around in as well.

Turtle decided that when the sun had warmed him a little, he would ask Squirrel to help him build as pleasant a home upon the ground.

He found his friend clinging to the far end of a branch with his wife scolding him from the other.

'May I ask you about a problem?' Turtle said.

'Gladly!' Squirrel replied. 'Gladly!' He jumped to another tree and ran down its trunk.

'And don't you dare go off anywhere without fixing it!' his wife called after him.

'What's the trouble?' Turtle asked with sympathy.

'She says I didn't build our house right and she has a stiff neck from the draught!' Squirrel grumbled. 'I wish she had a stiff jaw too! Then she couldn't complain so much! What's wrong with you?'

'I was just wishing that I had a winter home like yours,' Turtle admitted. 'But I guess yours isn't perfect, either.'

'Far from it!' Squirrel exclaimed. 'My wife and I can't get away from each other! If I had a nice big house like Raccoon's, I could live inside one branch and my wife inside another. I could store my seeds and nuts in it, too, so I wouldn't have to go out in the cold to get something to eat!'

'If Raccoon should give it up for any reason,' Turtle said, 'why couldn't you live in the branches and I live down among the roots?'

Then they looked at each other and smiled.

'If I had your brain,' Squirrel said, 'I could find a reason why he should give it to us.'

'And if I had your gift of speech,' Turtle told him, 'I would know how to talk him into it.'

'Then let's work together,' Squirrel suggested, 'and see what we can do.'

'Fine!' said Turtle. 'That tree doesn't look very safe to me.'

Squirrel laughed. 'I'll make him think it's going to fall over tomorrow!' he said.

So off they went that evening to the old maple in which Raccoon lived the year round. It was a splendid home for anyone, with three hollow branches and a huge, partly hollow trunk.

'Good evening,' Squirrel called.

Raccoon, who had just awakened, looked out of his window. 'Welcome!' he exclaimed. He thought that Squirrel was his friend. Besides, he was as polite as he was tidy. 'Welcome to you both!'

'Your house is what we want to talk to you about,' Squirrel explained. 'Turtle is so worried that he asked me to come over and see you.'

Raccoon studied both Squirrel and Turtle carefully. He was wiser than they thought. He could have been chief of all the raccoons if he had wanted to. Surely they didn't know that only last night he had found a dangerous crack on the thin side of the trunk and had picked out a new home? He decided that they were up to something. He decided to play as innocent as they.

'I'm very grateful for your interest,' he said to Turtle. 'What do you think is wrong with it?'

'Don't you know,' Squirrel said, 'that Bear chose this tree as his home but never moved in because he was sure that it would be blown down by the first bad winter wind?'

Raccoon pretended to be worried. 'No,' he said. 'He didn't tell me that.'

'Why don't you let me examine the different parts,' Squirrel offered, 'and find out whether it's safe?'

Raccoon remembered that the crack did not show through the bark. 'The children are still asleep,' he said. 'But if you could do it from the outside, that would be fine, although I'm afraid I can't pay you very much.'

This was a new thought to Squirrel. He had not expected to be paid. But what harm would it do to earn a little present by his trickery, as well as a new home?

'Oh, I wouldn't demand a payment from a friend,' he said. 'But of course it will take a lot of time and careful thought. So if you happen to know where you could get – let's say, about twenty walnuts or hickory nuts, it would keep my wife a little quieter.'

Raccoon did happen to know where there were twenty walnuts – right in one of Squirrel's own hiding places, which he had discovered by accident three days ago. And he saw no reason why he should pay Squirrel to look at a house which he was going to give up.

'Very well,' he answered, 'I'll deliver that number of walnuts when you have finished the job.'

Squirrel leapt up on to a stump happily. Then he studied Raccoon's tree from its crown to its roots, jerking his tail up and down as he did when he was excited. 'I certainly didn't think it was that bad!' he exclaimed.

'Bad in what way?' Raccoon asked.

'Look at it!' Squirrel exclaimed. 'It even leans toward the south. So when the north wind blows, it already has a head-start to the ground.'

'Oh, dear!' said Raccoon. 'And it has such lovely storage space.'

Squirrel climbed down solemnly. 'I'll do what repair work I can,' he offered, 'so it won't fall down right away. But I can't promise anything without charging you more nuts.'

'If I could get some help,' Raccoon asked, 'wouldn't it be much safer to move?'

At this Squirrel almost laughed out loud. 'It might be,' he agreed. 'Yes, it might. But where will you get the help?'

Raccoon was pretty sure that Squirrel had stored other pockets of nuts near the first one. So he made a new offer.

'I know a tree that might do,' he said. 'But I want a separate nest for every member of the family. Your teeth are sharper than mine. I'll give you twice the number of walnuts if you'll chew the nests out for me.'

110

'I think I could,' said Squirrel happily.

'And it would be much easier to do,' Raccoon said, 'if someone would take care of the children while my wife and I are making the beds more comfortable with grass and ferns.'

'I will make the new rooms,' Squirrel said. 'And Turtle and I will take turns watching the babies.'

Then Squirrel and Turtle said goodbye and left. All three were pleased with the bargain.

Turtle, however, was not quite as pleased as Squirrel. 'What good will twenty nuts do me?' he asked. 'Why didn't you demand ten nuts and ten fish?'

'Because I'm doing most of the work,' Squirrel said, 'and I don't like fish.'

'You *should* do most of the work!' Turtle pointed out. 'You will have most of the tree!'

'Let's not quarrel,' Squirrel said. 'We're both going to have a wonderful home for the winter.'

Squirrel did not love his work. Even with his sharp teeth, it was hard to cut out four nests from living wood. And, of course, his wife scolded him for being away so much. How glad he would be when the cold weather slowed down her tongue!

Raccoon, on the other hand, was so pleased that he dug up half of Squirrel's nuts and paid him these before he was through. Then he watched where Squirrel hid them and dug them up again for his second payment...

Then suddenly the north wind began to moan in the distance, and came down out of the hills, fleeing before the frost spirits. 'Hurry, hurry, hurry!' it moaned. 'It's cold, cold, cold!'

Raccoon did not have to hurry. He was settled now in a nice warm new home, paid for in full.

Squirrel thought that he too did not have to hurry. 'Now I will show you what I have been working at,' he said to his wife. 'You'll be sorry that you scolded me when you see our new home.' With a nut in his mouth, he led her from branch to branch toward the Raccoon's tree, which was now vacant and ready to be lived in.

They had barely started, however, when they heard a great crash in its direction.

'What was that?' his wife asked.

'It sounded like a tree,' he said in a voice quiet with fear.

They went on. They jumped from stone to stone across a narrow brook. They climbed a trunk to their natural paths again. Squirrel dreaded to look down. Then all too soon there was Raccoon's tree, twisted and broken, lying on the ground. Beside it lay Turtle, stunned.

'That's probably the tree we just heard,' Squirrel's wife said. 'Don't stop here! We must go on to our new home.'

Squirrel turned about unhappily and headed back toward their nest. 'That *was* our new home!' he said. 'We'll have to sleep close together tonight to keep warm.'

It is better to forget what his wife said.

And Turtle? He had lived a long time and knew that life held many disappointments. He recovered from the shock and went back to his pond. There he dug his way slowly into the mud.

The winter might be long. But at least he would pass it in peace.

Traditional North American Indian, retold by Roger Squire